The Little Boy Who Lived Down the Drain

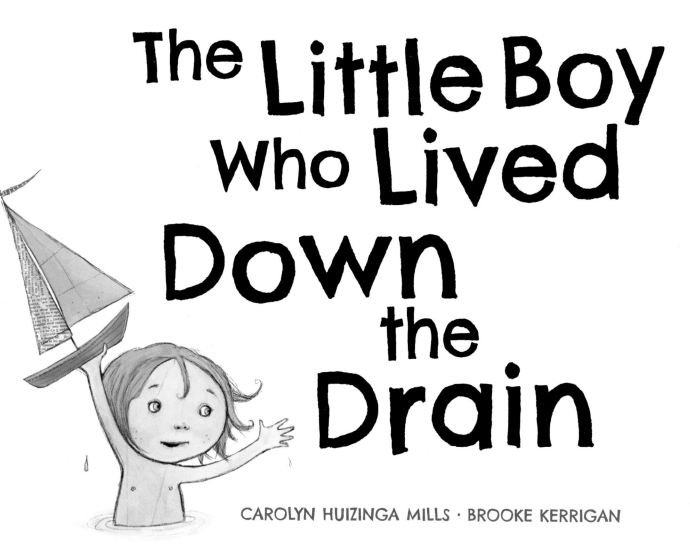

CAROLYN HUIZINGA MILLS · BROOKE KERRIGAN

Published in Canada by Fitzhenry & Whiteside Limited, 195 Allstate Parkway, Markham, ON L3R 4T8
Published in the United States by Fitzhenry & Whiteside Limited, 311 Washington Street, Brighton, MA 02135

www.fitzhenry.ca
10 9 8 7 6 5 4 3 2 1

Fitzhenry & Whiteside acknowledges with thanks the Ontario Arts Council for their support of our publishing program. We acknowledge the financial support of the Government of Canada through the Canada Book Fund (CBF) for our publishing activities.

Library and Archives Canada Cataloguing in Publication
Mills, Carolyn Huizinga, author
The Little Boy Who Lived Down The Drain / Carolyn Huizinga Mills; illustrated by Brooke Kerrigan. -- First edition.
ISBN 978-1-55455-395-2 (hardcover)
I. Kerrigan, Brooke, illustrator II. Title.
PS8626.I4563L58 2017   jC813'.6   C2017-902665-8

Publisher Cataloging-in-Publication Data (U.S.)
Names: Mills, Carolyn Huizinga, author. | Kerrigan, Brooke, illustrator.
Title: The Little Boy Who Lived Down the Drain /author, Carolyn Huizinga Mills ; illustrator, Brooke Kerrigan.
Description: Markham, Ontario : Fitzhenry & Whiteside Limited, 2017. | Summary: "Since learning that one of Baa Baa Black Sheep's three bags of wool went to the Little Boy Who Lived Down the Drain, Sally has wanted to meet him. Now, at every bath time, Sally talks with the Little Boy and discovers more about her new friend" – Provided by publisher.
Identifiers: ISBN 978-1-55455-395-2 (hardcover)
Subjects: LCSH: Baths -- Juvenile fiction. | Nursery rhymes. | BISAC: JUVENILE FICTION / Imagination & Play. | JUVENILE FICTION / Humorous Stories.
Classification: LCC PZ7.1M555Li | DDC [F] – dc23

Cover and text design by Brooke Kerrigan
Printed in China

For Hannah and Jacob
Whose imaginations are an unending source of inspiration
-C.H.M.

For John, with love
-B.K.

Sally loved taking baths. It wasn't because the water was full of soapy bubbles, although the soapy bubbles were nice. It wasn't because she had the bathroom all to herself, although that was nice too. And it wasn't because she came out squeaky clean, although she did like being squeaky clean.

Sally loved taking baths because she loved talking to the little boy who lived down the drain. He was the best listener in the whole world.

She discovered him one day after hearing her
mother singing to her bawling little brother:

Baa, baa, black sheep,
Have you any wool?
Yes sir, yes sir,
Three bags full.
One for the master,
One for the dame,
And one for the little boy ...

Who lives down the DRAIN.

Down the drain? How exciting! Sally
didn't know anybody else who lived down a
drain. There were so many things she wanted
to know. Where was the rest of his family?
Was he stuck there? What was he doing
with that bag of wool?

The next time Sally had a
bath, she also had a plan.
She waited until the end of
her bath, after all the water
had emptied out, and then she
leaned over the drain and shouted,
"HELLO! Can you hear me?"

HELLO

She waited and waited, but there was no answer. She shouted again, a little louder this time, "HELLO down there!"

"Sally!" her mother scolded, poking her head around the bathroom door. "What on earth are you doing in there? Stop making such a terrible racket and put on some pajamas before you freeze to death."

Reluctantly, Sally got ready for bed, but she didn't forget about the little boy who lived down the drain.

In fact, the very next time she had a bath, she had a new plan. Right below the tap in the bathtub, there was a round metal cover with a small opening in it. Laying flat on her stomach, she spoke directly into this opening.

"Hello?" she whispered. Then just a teensy bit louder (but not loud enough to make a terrible racket), she whisper-yelled, "Helllloooo!"

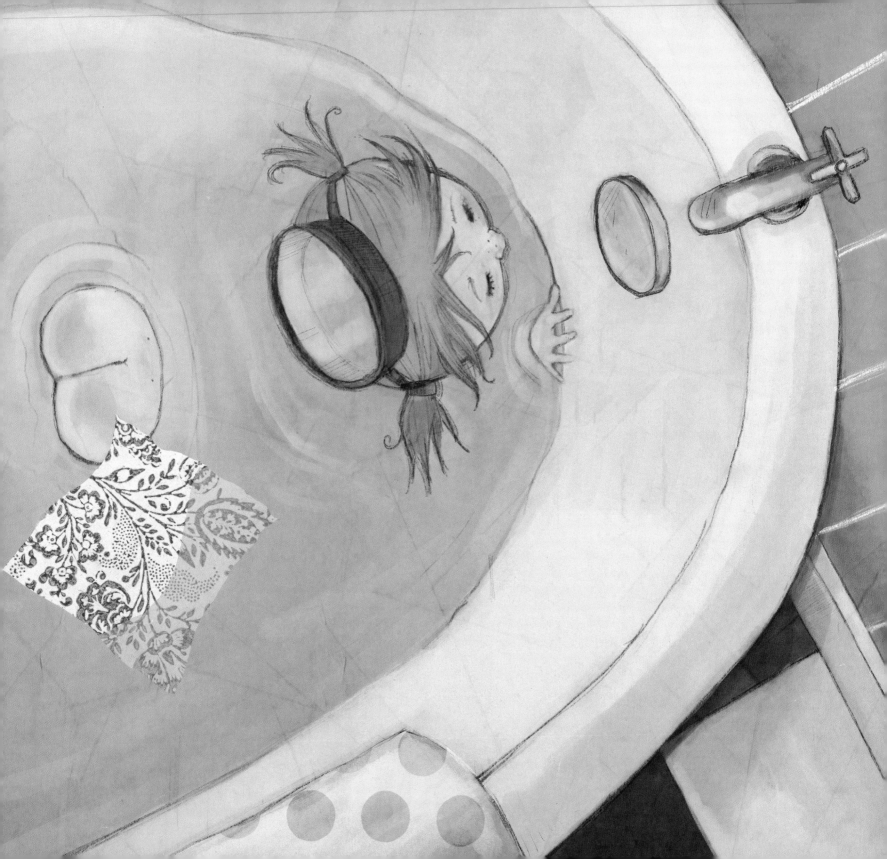

Her voice echoed, as if filling a large space — large enough for a little boy with a bag of wool to live.

"Hello, little boy. My name is Sally. Are you all by yourself down there? It must be very lonely having no one to talk to."

Sally could almost see the little boy sitting on a small stool in a big hollow room at the bottom of the drain. He was so little that his teeny-tiny voice was too teeny tiny for Sally to hear. So Sally did all the talking.

She talked about anything and everything that came into her head — from brussel sprouts to brain freezes — but she talked mostly about her family.

She grumbled about how her brother cried all the time. And how her sisters never let her play with them because she wasn't big enough. And how her parents didn't pay attention to her because they were always too busy.

"No one in my family listens," she complained. "You have no idea how annoying it is — my brother wailing whenever I try to talk, my sisters slamming their door in my face, my mom and dad saying, 'Not right now, not right now'. It's awful!"

Bath after bath, the little boy who
lived down the drain just listened. He
didn't interrupt.

He didn't argue with
her. He didn't laugh
at her.

He let her talk, and talk, and talk.

But after a while, Sally wanted to know what the little boy thought about all of this.

She pressed her ear tightly against the opening, but she couldn't hear him at all. She wished he could find a way to answer her. It was hard being the only one talking.

"Little boy, I just can't hear you!" she groaned, frustrated. She brought her mouth closer to the opening, cupped her hands around it, and said, "I know you're probably trying, but you need to try something different!"

To her surprise, Sally heard a teeny tiny voice cry back, "Try something different-rent-ent!"

Try something different? That gave Sally the most marvelous idea.

TRY SOMETHING DIFFERENT

The next time her brother cried all through breakfast and no one could hear anything she said, she stopped talking and shared a piece of her toast with him. He was quiet for forty-four seconds in a row.

When her sisters refused to let her play dress-up with them, she took out her two–hundred–and–fifty–eight–piece set of sidewalk chalk and invited them to draw with her. Together, they made very colourful creations.

And when her parents didn't have time to watch her practice her pirouettes or somersault across the living room, she stopped and watched what they were doing instead, like helping her sisters with the dishes, or changing her brother's diaper, or packing her lunch for school. Sally realized that much like her favourite toys, she had to share her parents, too.

Then, one morning, as she made funny faces at her baby brother, he stopped crying and actually smiled at her.

One afternoon, without being forced by anyone,
her sisters asked her to build a fort with them
and then even laughed at her jokes.

And one evening, her mother and father sat down with her, just the three of them, so she could read a story to them.

As the weeks went by, Sally stopped talking to the little boy who lived down the drain. She had too many other people to talk to instead. She wondered if he missed hearing her voice. She wondered if he was sad. She wondered if maybe she should start talking to him again.

A few nights later, while she was getting ready for bed, she heard her mother singing a familiar song:

Baa, baa, black sheep,
Have you any wool?
Yes sir, yes sir,
Three bags full.
One for the master,
One for the dame,
And one for the little boy…

Who lives down the LANE.

Down the lane? What a relief!
Sally didn't need to worry about
not talking to the little boy who
lived down the drain anymore.

He had moved.